LOST
ON THE
ROAD
TO
NOWHERE

by
Scott Fowler

Dedication:

*To the real Chapel, Salem, London and Georgia Fowler,
who provided the inspiration for this book.
I am proud to be your Dad.*

TABLE OF CONTENTS

CHAPTER 1

THE DEER

I saw the deer before anybody else did, standing in the middle of the road like she was just waiting for our car to run over her. Behind her stood a fawn on wobbly legs. I remember seeing the white spots on the fawn's back and thinking for a second they were snowflakes.

I saw them both first, because I was the only one paying much attention to the road. Salem and London were fighting in the third row of our minivan. The baby, Georgia, was crying in the middle row right beside me. Mom was telling Dad he should have stayed on the main road instead of taking this sort-of-illegal shortcut that he kept bragging was a road no one even knew about anymore since the new highway had gone in. "It doesn't feel like a shortcut," Mom said. "It feels like a road to nowhere."

It didn't seem like it was late afternoon on Christmas Eve right then. There was no peace on earth in our van, and not much goodwill toward men, either. But that's what it was. That's why we were on this road trip in the first place. We were going toward my grandparents' house for a Christmas holiday in the North Carolina mountains. We had been thinking about how cool it would be to have a white Christmas if it snowed – none of us had seen snow for a couple of years.

Dad started yelling at Salem and London, trying to make them be quiet. He also kept trying to reach back with his right hand to find Georgia's doll on the floor so he could hand it back up to her and calm her down. It was what Mom likes to call "Everyday Chaos." She says that's what she's going to call her blog if she ever has time to write one.

We have a family of six – two parents, four kids. When we go into a restaurant, people look at us funny and sometimes ask if they can sit a little further away. My name is Chapel. I'm 11 years old and I am the oldest, so I try not to get into all the arguing that my two younger brothers do. But sometimes I can't help it because they are so totally wrong about so many things. Arguing is one of our family traditions, like reading bedtime stories or fighting over who gets the biggest piece of pumpkin pie.

No one argues with me now about who saw the deer first, though. I don't know why. Maybe they just know that I did, because I was the one who yelled "Look!" Or maybe it's just because it doesn't seem as important to us now, because so much happened after the deer – so many things that will change our family forever.

Now when I think about those 18 hours right after the deer walked onto that road, I can't believe it all happened. Not to us. We were just an ordinary family -- a little bigger than most, but otherwise not that unusual. We live in a small town called Denver, N.C. No, not Denver, Colorado. Our Denver doesn't ever get snow, and it doesn't have any mountains, and it's so small that every time we go into a restaurant, my mom or dad always know someone and have an extremely long and boring talk with them. My dad works 30 miles away at the newspaper in Charlotte, writing about city council meetings and school boards and a lot of other stuff I don't understand and don't want to.

My mom met my dad at the newspaper on the escalator. "Between the second and third floors, going down," they always say. Then he proposed to her on the same escalator a few months later, late one night when they sneaked back into the building. Then they got married a few months after that.

Then they started having a baby every three years, like they set a clock for it or something. After there were two of us kids, Mom quit working and started taking care of us all the time. She says she likes taking care of us better than any job she could have. But sometimes when she says it, her face is kind of pinched, like she just bit into a lemon.

But nothing much exciting had happened to our family since I was born. Having a new baby brother or sister every three years was about as good as it got. I was always reading these adventure stories in the library about kids who find out they are wizards, or kids who solve mysteries, or kids who suddenly develop superpowers. We weren't like that. We were just kids. And we were pretty much minding our own business until that deer and her baby walked onto the road.

My dad looked when I yelled, "Watch out!" Then he swung the wheel way too far to one side. Dad had never let me drive a car, not even for one second in the big field behind our house, but even I knew that what Dad did to that steering wheel wasn't quite right. I have watched him drive a lot, and I had never seen him yank it like that, like he was trying to tear it off completely. Then my Mom screamed. And I had

never heard her scream like that before, like she knew
how badly she and Dad were going to get hurt before
it even happened. And a few seconds after that, there
was a lot of blood. I don't really like to think about the next part. I
don't like to think about a bunch of those 18 hours,
really, even though not everything that happened was
bad. But it's like I have to think about it. My mind
won't let me forget. And some parts I like to think
about. Some parts, I'm proud of.

Do you know that deer and her baby walk through
my dreams sometimes? I'll be having a perfectly nor-
mal dream about a test in social studies class, where
we had to memorize all the states and their capitals.
Mrs. Zappone will have called on me to recite them
all, and I know I know them, so I'm not nervous. But
I'll be in my rhythm, just getting past all those "M"
states – Jackson, Mississippi; Jefferson City, Missouri;
Helena, Montana -- when the deer and her fawn walk
through the door to the classroom and right up to
the front of Mrs. Zappone's class and just stare at
me. The deer and her fawn never say anything – they
gaze at me with those huge deer eyes, and sometimes
somebody behind me yells "Look!" and then I usually
wake up.

Since it doesn't look like I'm going to forget those
18 hours anytime soon, I decided I'm going to write
them down instead. I think getting it on paper or in a

computer will get it out of my mind, and maybe get those deer out of my dreams. It's a little spooky when the deer walk in to Mrs. Zappone's class, to tell you the truth. I wish they would talk or something. I'd like to know what they want.

We didn't kill the deer, you know. Neither one of them. They're probably out in those same woods right now, doing whatever it is deer do. Looking for berries or something. But before I get to the wreck and what happened after that, I need to tell you a little more about our family, so maybe you'll understand a little more why we did everything the way we did it.

CHAPTER 2

THE FAMILY

Let me back up a little. My full name is Chapel Scott Fowler. I'm eleven years old and in the 5th grade, even though I've been going to school six years. They don't count kindergarten as a grade — it's just like it's for practice or something. That's a total rip-off. I like school OK, although I'd never admit that to my parents. But I hated one part of kindergarten — the fact they made you lie down for 20 minutes of quiet time every day. Another total rip-off. I'm taller than everybody but one girl in my fifth-grade class, and I like to wear my hair as long as my Mom and the school dress code will allow. I hate when people ask me what I want to be when I grow up, although I'll tell them "comic book illustrator" sometimes just so they won't ask anymore. I love to build Lego sets, too – I can follow the directions for those a lot quicker than either of my parents can. If the set has fewer than 300 pieces, I don't consider it much of a challenge.

I don't really know what I'm good at yet except for drawing and spelling. I love to spell. I have finished in the top three of my classroom spelling bee each of the past three years, and two years straight I won it. Usually, if I see a new word and look at it a couple of times, it just sticks in my mind and flashes inside there in red letters, like a sign for a restaurant at night.

In fifth grade, we switch classes and teachers every hour, which is a lot better than the other grades, where you had to stay in one place. There, if you get a teacher you don't like – too bad. You're stuck with her for seven hours a day. My younger brother Salem has it that way now – he's in second grade. One teacher only, all day long. He likes his teacher, though. She likes him, too, Mom said. The teacher told Mom that Salem is a true gentleman. It's obvious his teacher has no idea how he acts at home.

Salem is eight years old. He's got long brown hair like me, but he's a lot shorter than I am. And more athletic, too. He can beat me in "H-O-R-S-E" on our backyard basketball goal most of the time. He learned how to swim before I did. He tries things I would never attempt. The first time he tried to do a front flip off my parents' bed, I saw it. He had never done one before. So he just thought about how he might do it for a few seconds inside his head, he said. Then he bounced a couple of times, did a real somersault in the air (the word "somersault" put Collin Jones out in the spelling bee last year, by the way) and landed on his feet on the carpet.

Mom walked in right as he jumped. She had a laundry basket of clean clothes under her arm, and she dropped it on the ground and yelled "Salem!" She said later she just about had a heart attack. She told him never to do it again, but he still does it sometimes when he knows Mom and Dad aren't around.

The youngest brother in our family is London, who just turned five and has red hair. He doesn't go to school yet because he's too young and I think he is very spoiled. His red hair is really thick and every grown-up woman wants to put their hand on his head or squeeze his cheeks. He has been told so often that he's "cuter than the average boy" that when he was three he asked Mom and Dad who the Abrage boy was anyway and where he lived.

London likes to scream a lot when we only annoy him a little bit, which we only do for his own good. He needs to be tough if he's going to make it through kindergarten starting next school year. He likes to say, whenever we do something just a tiny bit bad, "Get Chapel and Salem *immediately* in trouble!" Mom and Dad always take his side, even though he won't do any clean-up when we're supposed to work together to be able to watch TV that night. And he still gets to watch TV, too, although he used to always be afraid of this one monster on a Chef Boyardee commercial, so for a long time he wouldn't watch any TV show because he never could be sure that monster wouldn't show up on a commercial.

That was OK with me — then we didn't have to fight over the two good chairs in the bonus room. London and I don't fight much — we are six years apart — but Salem and London fight all the time. Once Salem scratched London on the arm hard enough to bleed and got in trouble for it. His argument to Mom and Dad that his punishment shouldn't be severe was this: "It's not my fault! He has weak skin!"

London can be very brave when he really wants to be — he slept with all the lights off before any of us did. But he has to be motivated. One time, in this story I'm going to tell you, he was braver than anyone I've ever seen in my life. But I still think he's a little spoiled.

None of us three brothers like girls much. We make only two exceptions to that rule. The first is our cousin, Paige. She's cool. She's 11 and she's great at soccer and she and I write scary stories together sometimes. But we don't see her much – she lives a long way away.

As for girls that live nearby, we don't like any of them. We have this small clubhouse at my grandparents' house that they let us build with old boards and other stuff we found in the woods. On the biggest board, we painted a sign that said, "No Girls Allowed." I wanted to spell "girls" with a "z" because it looks cooler that way, but Dad said no.

Well, there actually is one girl nearby we all like. She's the second exception. She is our baby sister. Her name is Georgia, and she's 19 months old. She is extremely cute and likes to pick out her own clothes already, which Dad says is funny now but will be a problem later. She will get in the closet she shares with Mom and Dad and say "No no" to everything until they get to something she likes, and then she goes, "Dat dat dat." She loves stripes, so if you just skip straight to the clothes with stripes on them, you can avoid a lot of wasted time.

Georgia can say about 20 words, including "Mama," "Dada," "bye bye," "bubbles," "hock (which means sock)," "bubba (which means brother)," "car," "kay (which means OK)," "candy," backpack" and "no no." "No no" is her second-favorite word. She says it to all of us brothers all the time, because she's a terrible sharer. If she grabs something we are playing with, we are not allowed to get it back. Her very favorite word, though, is "helmet." She has a blue bike helmet that is toddler-sized, and she likes to wear it all the time. She will wake up in the morning and say "helmet, helmet" and pat her head, and until you get it for her, she will drive you crazy wanting it. So a lot of times we just let her wear the helmet when she's wandering around the house. Mom says it won't hurt her.

Georgia had on her helmet when I saw the deer. She had been wearing it practically the whole car trip – it was the only way Dad could get her to calm down and get back in her car seat. She had worn it inside the gas station when we had gotten a ton of snacks after Dad pumped the gas. That's one good thing about our family on road trips – we buy all sorts of junk food that we don't usually get at home. Dad did make us all go to the gross gas-station bathroom, though, even when we all said we didn't need to – another total rip-off. And then it hadn't even snowed yet, even though the sky was gray and it was plenty cold – yet another total rip-off.

Georgia had worn the helmet back to the car after going into the gas station. She ate her tiny cheese crackers, and since she ate them very slowly, that kept her occupied for awhile. But then she decided she had had enough of the car ride, which was a problem because it was still two more hours to my grandparents' house in the North Carolina mountains. That's even with the shortcut my Dad took, which he really wasn't supposed to do. He circled around a metal gate and a big "Road Closed" sign, with black letters painted on an orange background, to get on the road we were on. He said it was safe and that he knew where it went because he had used to drive on it all the time and had heard from "somebody," although he forgot who exactly, that it was still a good road that no one used. He also said it would save us at least 30 minutes, and given the way Georgia was behaving that we would need every minute of that.

So that brings us up to when Dad was trying to reach down on the floor of the minivan – to get Georgia her doll. My parents freak out sometimes when the baby starts crying, like it's the first time they've heard one do it or something. They've had four kids by now, so you'd think they would be used to it. I sure am. I was sitting in the middle row of the van, beside Georgia, because it gets too cramped when you put the three of us boys all in the third row in the back.

Meanwhile, London and Salem were screaming at each other. They were just bored, that's all. London said that Salem had touched his hair when there was supposed to be no touching at all, and Salem said touching hair didn't count because if you touched it real lightly, the other person couldn't even feel it.

Then London had whacked Salem on his own head and said, "Do you feel that?" And Salem had hit London on the shoulder and London had cried and yelled: "Get Salem *immediately* in trouble." And Dad had said in his sternest voice from the front: "What did you do to him, Salem?" while he was reaching for Georgia's doll, Miss Peggy. Mom had given Miss Peggy the doll her name, because Georgia wanted to call the doll "No No" and she already has three other dolls named "No No." I could have reached the doll easier than he could have, but he didn't ask me.

That's when the deer walked out on the road, and I said "Look!" and Dad swung the wheel way too far. And that's when all of our little problems turned into one big problem.

CHAPTER 3

THE WRECK

I could tell we were going to miss hitting the deer as soon as Dad yanked the wheel. And we did. I saw the deer one more time as we went by, but this time from a different window, because the car was spinning. The fawn's white spots were a blur. Mom was screaming and Georgia was crying but all of us brothers were quiet. Salem and London stopped fighting immediately – they were not bored anymore. Dad was trying to do something with the steering wheel. My heart felt weird, like it was trying to jump out of my chest.

I don't know how many times the van spun around. But then it felt like it was going straight down, like the first drop on the old "Thunder Road" rollercoaster at Carowinds, the one my Dad likes so much because he says it is "old school." I love rollercoasters, too, but this time I was just scared. I knew it wasn't right. We bumped over something so hard that my head nearly hit the ceiling. And then I heard a huge BAM!! At the same time, the car stopped with such a jolt that my head hit Mom's seat right in front of me.

Everything was quiet for one second. Maybe two. It was like the air had all been sucked out of our bodies. And then everyone drew in a breath and it was real, real loud. I could hear Mom and Georgia and Salem and London in the back, and I think I was yelling "What happened? What happened?" but I'm not sure what I said. What I couldn't figure out was that it looked like two huge tree trunks had now taken the place of my parents and were sitting in the front seats of the car. I could barely see Mom or Dad. What I mostly saw were those trees. They were pine trees, I could tell, because some of the nee-dles on a few of the branches had actually reached in through the front window. And the car's dark gray dashboard looked strange, too, like a giant had shoved it straight down into the car. The dashboard actually looked like it had jammed into both of my parents' stomachs.

The van was old. I don't know how old, but older than I am. It was made sometime in the 1990s, I know that. My parents had bought it used to carry us around once there were four of us. I knew it didn't have any airbags, because Mom had told me a few weeks ago that we were going to get a new van that did pretty soon. We just hadn't gotten around to it yet, she said, because Dad had been working so much and hadn't had time to look. Plus, they needed to save a little more money first, she had said.

The first thing I did was touch my head, because I was afraid it was bleeding. It wasn't, but I saw a lot of blood in the front seat and it was coming from somewhere. Then I looked at Georgia, who was still crying her head off but still buckled into her pink car seat, which looked the same as it always does. I could still see her blue helmet. There was a pine needle stuck to it. Then I heard Mom. "Boys?" she said, and it came out almost like a whisper, not like the way she usually talks when she wants to get her attention. "Boys? Are you OK?"

"I'm OK, Mom," I said. I unbuckled my seat belt and looked back at my brothers. London was crying. Salem looked terrified. "Are you hurt?" I said. And they just looked at me kind of weird and I said again, louder, "Are you hurt?" Salem shook his head, staring at me with eyes that looked as big as those on the deer. London kept crying, but a little softer. I didn't see anything wrong with either of them.

"Everyone be quiet for a second," I said. For once they listened to me. "I need to talk to Mom." Then I turned back toward her.

"I think they're OK, Mom," I said, and I tried to make my voice strong, because she sounded sad or hurt. Or both. "And the baby is OK."

But the car was a mess. I could tell that from where I sat. It's like the first row of seats had totally disappeared. The hood had buckled. One of the side doors was halfway off, too. There was broken glass everywhere.

"Oh," Mom said, and it came out kind of like a moan. "OK, honey." There was a long pause. Then she said "Boys, are you OK?" Like the last few seconds hadn't even happened.

I started again, "I think…"

But she interrupted me and said some more words. Georgia had stopped crying by then, so I heard her clearly. "I love you all," she whispered. "Your Dad and I love you all so much."

"We know," I said. I don't like when anyone talks about love. Do people have to say things like that all the time?

"What do we need to do?" I asked her. "Is Dad OK? Will the car go?" There were so many questions

I wanted to ask. But she didn't say anything back. Then her eyes closed.

"Dad," I said. "Dad?? What do we need to do?"

Dad didn't say anything, either. I tried to push past the branches of the pine tree and find him in what had been the driver's seat. And I did, but I wished that I hadn't. He had blood all over the forehead. His mouth was open. His eyes were closed. I put my hand up to his mouth and felt the breath coming out, but he looked really hurt. I shook him by the shoulder and I patted his cheek, first lightly and then harder. But he didn't do anything. I couldn't even see his legs because the pine needles, the trees and the dashboard were messing up everything.

I could see a little more of Mom when I turned to my right. She had blood on her, too, but not quite as much. I took her shoulder and shook her a little and while I was doing that, I had an idea. What about a cell phone? I didn't have one yet – although a lot of kids in my class did – but both my parents usually carried one. We could call for help on that.

"Mom?" I said. "Mom?" She opened her eyes and looked at me again. At first, she seemed like she was staring at my hair. But then her eyes focused on me, and I could tell she was really looking at me again, and that made me feel happier for a second. She looked at Dad, and then at the smashed front of the car.

"Mom, do you know where your cell phone is?" I asked.

"I didn't bring it," she said, and she sounded like she was about to cry. "I left it at home in the charger."

"What about Dad?" I persisted.

"I don't know," she said. "Maybe. You can check. He usually keeps it in his front right pocket."

I snaked my hand around a tree branch and under the dashboard and managed to find the pocket of Dad's blue jeans. Yes! I could feel the phone in there. I pulled it out quickly – or at least I thought I did. Only half of it came out – the top half. It had broken in two. I pulled out the other half, too, trying to see if somehow the two halves could be taped together or something, but the display screen was totally cracked. The power button didn't work at all when I mashed it a couple of times.

"Can you wake your Dad up?" Mom said, trying to move her head to see what I was doing.

"No," I said. "His phone's broken, and something's wrong with him."

"Something's wrong with me, too," she said, looking down at where the dashboard jammed into her stomach. "I can't move one of my legs."

"Do you want me to get you out?" I said. But when I looked at where she was and all the car parts and branches that had circled around her like a spider's web, I knew I would need a lot of help.

are going on a walk. Maybe it will even snow. That'll be fun, won't it?"

"Even Georgia?" London said, and he smiled a little. Like all of us, he loved Georgia.

"Even Georgia," I said. "I'm going to carry her in her backpack."

Georgia suddenly said: "Backpack!" She loved the backpack. My dad carried her in it all the time, especially when we took a family walk.

"Yes," Salem said, and suddenly I knew he had turned it around and was going to be a big help on this. He understood what was going on. He knew we were in a mess. The two younger ones hadn't realized it yet, but he knew. "We're going on a family walk, Georgia. You're going to ride in the backpack!"

Then, to me, he said: "Let's get out all the suitcases, Chapel. We should put on our snow stuff. All of it."

"How long is our walk?" London said. "I'm going to get hungry soon." London liked to make sure he told everyone he was going to be hungry in advance.

"That's a good idea, London," I said. "We'll bring snacks."

"And bottled water, too," Salem said. "There are a lot of them still in the back." He was getting into it now — I think he had forgotten for a second about Mom and Dad.

"We'll bring some of the bottled water and the food," I said, "but we need to put some of that by Mom and Dad, too. So Mom can reach it, and Dad too if he wakes up."

"Why is Dad asleep?" London asked, but I pretended not to hear.

I unbuckled Georgia from her car seat and pulled her toward me. Her helmet accidentally bonked me in the head. "Backpack!" she said. We all climbed out the door that had gotten knocked half off the car. Then we opened up the trunk and started digging into everything we could find.

There was an old blanket at the bottom of the trunk, just like Mom had said. I crawled back in the car and draped that around the pine branches and on top of Mom and Dad as best I could. I tucked it in around them. Neither of them moved.

I took some of their extra clothes and their big coats and stuffed those all around their shoulders and their heads, too, sort of like I was making a bed with them inside it. I didn't want London or Salem doing any of that, so I got them to entertain Georgia for a couple of minutes.

Then I unzipped one suitcase that had all of our snow gear in it, and luckily Mom had done a good packing job. We all had one good snow outfit apiece — most of them hand-me-downs from older cousins — as well as gloves and some boots and hats that fit us and weren't too hard to get on. We put the hats and gloves in our jacket pockets for later, but we skipped the boots except for Georgia's pink ones she liked so much. All of us boys preferred walking in our tennis shoes. It wasn't snowing, so I thought that would be OK.

London even got his snowsuit on mostly by himself, even though whenever Mom or Dad is around, he likes to make them do it. Salem had his school backpack in the car – he had forgotten to take it out after the last day of school before Christmas break. We unpacked all the books and school things he had in it and then repacked it with all the water and snacks it could hold.

We got Georgia into her snow stuff last. The pants were black and the coat was white, with a hood. We didn't pull up the hood, though, because of her blue helmet, so the hood just flopped back behind her. Then I put her in the backpack and buckled up the straps and loaded her up onto my shoulders. I tried to talk to Mom and Dad one more time, but they both seemed like they were going to be asleep a long time. That's what I told myself, anyway. They were just asleep under a blanket. That was all – nothing worse than that.

"I want to kiss them before we leave," Salem said. London said he wanted to also. They had a hard time reaching Mom and Dad's faces, but they crawled in there and did it. I didn't want to do that, and no one was there to tell me to, so I didn't.

"Their cheeks are cold," London said. He didn't say anything about the blood, and I didn't bring it up. We stood beside the van for a few seconds. I knew I needed to be the leader, but it was hard to think of what to say. Even though I was the oldest, I was used to Mom or Dad being in charge.

Salem actually spoke first once we were out of the van for good. "We should pray to God," he said.

"OK," I said. "You do it."

I thought he would argue, but he didn't.

"Dear God: Keep Mom and Dad safe until we find help," Salem said. "Amen."

"And keep Georgia safe," London added. "God is great, God is good, let us thank Him for this food…"

"Amen," I said, cutting him off before he started reciting all the prayers he had learned in Bible School last summer. "OK, good. Now listen – do you see these tracks?"

They all looked where I was pointing, at the tracks that ended at our back tires but dug a clear trench through old snow and mud down the hill. We had gone a long way down that hill before banging into the pine trees. It had to be at least half the size of a football field. "We're going to follow these, and then we'll get back on the road, and then we're going to find help for Mom and Dad."

"Who's going to help us?" London said.

"Someone will, London," Salem said, wiping a few leftover cracker crumbs from the corner of Georgia's mouth. "They will see Georgia and they won't be able to resist such a cute baby."

"That's right," I said, and started walking up the hill. Now that we were doing this, I wanted to get going. Fast. "Someone will help us — isn't that right, Georgia?"

"No no no," Georgia said happily. She had no idea what was happening. She just knew she was out of the car, which was exactly where she had wanted to be.

We followed the tire tracks back up the hill and set off down the road, the same way the car had been heading before the deer came.

CHAPTER 5

THE ROAD TO NOWHERE

We started off fine. The road was paved and easy to find. The tire tracks through the old snow that fell long before we had gotten here made it clear which direction Mom wanted us to go – away from the way we came. Georgia felt light in the backpack. Salem had the school backpack loaded with the drinks and snacks, along with three diapers and a few wipes for Georgia.

"Ugh," he said when I had put the diapers in there. "Who's going to change her?"

"I will," London volunteered. "I can do it. I've seen Mom."

"We'll see," I said, which was an old trick of Mom and Dad's when they weren't ready to make a decision quite yet. I couldn't believe London had volunteered before Salem and me, though. Sometimes he surprised me.

We started walking, but I could see from the way Salem was moving that he was getting "his energy going," as he likes to say.

"Do you think we should run?" Salem said. "Maybe I should run on up ahead a little and see if there are any houses. Then I'll run right back if there aren't."

I went ahead and let him do that, because the road was so straight I could see him the whole way. Salem would run up ahead for about 100 yards, then come back to us. He did it a lot faster than I could have, even if I hadn't had Georgia strapped to my back.

"Nothing but more woods," he'd say when he came back. Then he'd walk for awhile, get antsy and do it again. But after about five times with no luck, he settled down and just walked beside us.

It was like walking in the woods, really. The road cut right through a forest of huge pine and oak trees, a few of which still had their leaves.

We walked right down the middle of the road. It was still late afternoon and we wanted any car that came along to see us.

But there didn't seem to be any chance of that. I was no Encyclopedia Brown, but it was easy to see that this road was hardly ever used. Mom's "road to nowhere" nickname for it was pretty appropriate. There was no litter on the side of the road, for one thing. Not a Styrofoam cup. Not a hamburger wrapper. Not a bottle cap for the collection that we keep together in a Ziploc bag at home in a drawer. Nothing. And in places the trees had grown back up really close to the road, almost like they were slowly reclaiming their territory. There were pine needles scattered all over the road. A lot of times it looked like two cars would have trouble passing each other side by side if they were going in different directions.

We fell into a pattern. I went first, with Georgia in the backpack behind me. Salem was second when he wasn't running ahead to see what was coming next. London was third.

"How long do we have to walk?" Salem said after about half an hour.

I was wondering that myself. But I tried to think about what Dad would say to a question like that. "As long as it takes," I said.

"No no," Georgia said, joining the conversation. I sometimes forgot for a few minutes that she was even in the backpack. She was always so content back there that she often just looked at the scenery and wouldn't say anything as long as she was comfortable.

I had my watch with me, so I knew we had started walking at 3:30 p.m. I had just started wearing one because I wanted to know how much longer it was at school until math class was over. I couldn't stand math class.

After we had walked about an hour, a light snow began to fall. It cheered us up, because it was so rare to us, and we all tried to catch a few snowflakes on our tongue. Snow hadn't gotten us out of school for two years. The only time it had snowed in the past two years was on a weekend, and it was only there a couple of hours in the morning before it got hot again. It wasn't a good snow for snowmen or snowballs, either – it hadn't packed together right or something. By noon that day, almost all the snow had melted. That had been a total rip-off.

But this looked like it would be a good snow – it was already sticking on the road and in the trees' branches. Mom loves to take pictures, especially of us. It would have been a great place to shoot our annual Christmas card – the one I try hard never to smile for – except for what we had to do.

"What's going to happen to Mom and Dad?" London asked from the back. "Will the snow make them too cold?"

"They'll be fine," I said, trying to act more confident than I really felt. "They're going to be warm enough to be OK with all those blankets. The top of the van is OK. And they've got water."

"But what if they don't wake up?" asked Salem, drawing alongside me.

"They will," I said. "We just need to get them to a hospital. They have all kinds of medicine there that can wake them up."

But how were we going to do that? I kept wondering to myself. I knew that my dad told me once that a grown man walking normally could go three miles an hour. I figured we were going slightly slower than that – maybe two miles an hour. So it had been an hour. We had walked two miles and seen nothing but woods. No signs at all that any human lived around here, or for that matter had even gone down this road for a long time.

"I don't want to see any bears," London said. "I'm scared of bears."

"We're not going to see any bears," I said.

"OK," London said. "But I'm hungry."

I was, too, and I figured the baby might be. "OK," I said. "Salem, stop for a second. Open your backpack. Everyone can have one snack and we'll share one of the bottled waters, too."

We had four bottled waters altogether – we had started this trip off with a 12-pack, which I knew because I had to lug it out to the car when we left home. But we had already drunk five of those on the car trip. Of the seven remaining, I had decided we would take four and had left the other three for Mom and Dad.

"I want some Combos," Salem said.

"Ritz Bits," London said.

"Candy," Georgia said. She had been listening. Then she said it again, to make sure we understood. "Caaan-deee."

"OK," I said to all of them. "We'll eat and walk at the same time."

Salem and I passed out the treats. We gave Georgia a sucker – the flat kind Mom always gave to her, so she wouldn't choke. "Bank suckers," we called them, because they were the kind the lady at the drive-thru bank window always passed out.

"How many do you need?" she would ask Mom, holding up the suckers and trying to look back through the window to see how many of us were in there. The lady always seemed slightly startled when Mom asked for five – she liked bank suckers, too.

Not as much as Georgia, though. We handed her the sucker – it was green – and she gladly went to work on it.

"Mmmm," she said. "Mmmm." Of all of us, she was the happiest one. She didn't know what was going on. She just knew she was getting candy, and a walk, and a lot of attention from her three brothers.

"Does she need changing?" London asked.

I should have thought of that, but I hadn't. "She probably does," I admitted. "I don't think Mom changed her at the gas station. Let's stop for a second."

I took the backpack off and then lifted Georgia out. Salem shrugged off his coat and put it on the ground. And London, true to his word, got Georgia out of her snow pants and pink boots, took off the wet diaper and put on a new one. I didn't have to help him at all. He did a good job with it. I have a hard time with compliments sometimes, though, especially if it involves something one of my brothers do well. So I just patted him on the shoulder as he zipped Georgia back up.

"Londy!" Georgia said. "Londy! Tank! Tank!"

"She's saying 'Thank you,' London," Salem said, and London smiled. Salem helped me get Georgia back into the backpack. And we headed on.

CHAPTER 6

THE SLED

B y 5 p.m., we had all put on our gloves – I had to bend down so Salem could put on Georgia's without me having to take off the backpack again. I started to wish that we had put on our snow boots, too, back at the van, instead of sticking with our tennis shoes.

You could still see, but it was starting to get dark. We had maybe an hour of light left. Or less. It was also getting colder. And the snow was getting heavier – there was probably 2-3 inches of it on the road by now. And we didn't have a flashlight. Dad may have had one in the car, now that I thought about it, but I didn't know where it was and it was too late now.

I wondered how long we could walk in the dark. Since it was so cloudy, the moon and stars probably wouldn't help us much.

My brothers were dragging a little, so I tried to interest them in a game we sometimes played in the car. It's called "Would You Rather?" The point is to give the other person two terrible alternatives and make them choose one — my Dad said grown-ups would call it the lesser of two evils.

"OK," I said… "Would you rather eat a black banana that you found at the bottom of a sandbox or eat two handfuls of mud from the bottom of a pond?"

"The mud," London said, "because it wouldn't be so rotten." He thought for a second.

"Would you rather jump off the top of the Empire State Building or stand on top of Mt. Everest in only your underwear?"

"The Empire State Building," Salem said, "because I'd bring a hang glider with me. Now…. let me think…"

I knew what was coming. Salem's "Would You Rathers?" always involved bodily functions.

"OK," he said. "Would you rather sneeze out your butt or fart out your nose?"

"Sneeze out my butt," London said, and we all laughed. "Now it's my turn again. Would you rather..."

We went on like that for awhile until we climbed to the top of a pretty steep hill. Then London asked: "What's that?"

He was pointing to something on the side of the road in a ditch.

It looked like a long, straight, silver sheet of metal. If you had stood it on one end, it probably would have been about the size of a door, but a little skinnier.

"I don't know," I said. "But unless it can help us, we're not stopping." I kept walking.

"No no," Georgia said. "Londy! Londy!"

I glanced over my shoulder at her in the backpack, and London hadn't moved. Not only that, but Salem had stopped and was looking at the metal sheet, too.

"Maybe this can help us," Salem said slowly, and you could almost see the idea form above his head, like it was in a cartoon bubble. "Do you think we could all ride it down the hill?"

"Awesome!" London said. "Like a sled!"

I looked at the hill we were about to walk down. It was long and gradual – maybe three football fields worth of distance in all. "No, I don't..." I started to say, because it is my habit to disagree with most ideas my brothers have. I know I am disagreeable sometimes. I just can't seem to help it.

But then I stopped. They had been walking a long way. We hadn't seen any signs of another person yet, and it wouldn't hurt us to maybe have a bit of fun if it didn't take but a minute. Enough snow now covered the road that maybe the makeshift sled would work. Georgia still had her helmet on, too, which I was glad of because it was keeping her warm. I walked back a few steps to take a closer look at it. Maybe Salem and London actually had a good idea here.

"I think maybe it's supposed to be part of a tin roof," I said. "I don't know what it's doing here. Maybe it fell off a truck."

"Who cares what it's doing here?" Salem asked. "Let's ride it – just down that hill. For fun."

"All four of us?" I asked, still doubtful.

"Yes," he said. "The four of us. The Fowler Four. C'mon, Chapel. You know it will be faster. Aren't you tired of walking?"

"Yeah, yeah!" London chimed in. "The Fowler Four! On a sled! If you don't do it, Chapel, I'll get you *immediately* in trouble!" He jumped while he told this small joke, the bangs of his red hair bouncing against his forehead.

"OK," I said. "We'll try. But if it goes too fast, I'm putting my feet down and stopping us."

We all worked to pull the sheet of tin out of the ditch and onto the top of the hill. It had a lot of dirt caked on it – it had been there awhile. While we were pulling it out and brushing it off, I looked at the large pine tree that part of the piece of tin had leaned up against. Three parallel lines sliced down the center of the tree's trunk, a little higher than I could reach, maybe six feet up. They were deep cuts, too. I wondered briefly what could have made them. And it looked like there were a couple of jet-black woolly worms or something stuck to the bark of the tree, too. Maybe it wasn't worms. Maybe it was hair. Or feathers. Or fur. I didn't have time to think about that, though – not with everyone so hot to ride our homemade sled.

I got on first, sitting at the very back, with Georgia still in the backpack behind me. She was patting my back over and over – she does that sometimes when she is excited or nervous. London got on next, right in front of me, and then Salem got in the very front, since he wanted so much to do it. I was surprised that he did, really, because he never wants to ride the rollercoasters at Carowinds.

"Here we go," I said, pushing off with my hands and feet.

At first, I didn't think we were going to move at all. The front of the sled was digging right through the snow and into the road instead of sliding over the top of it. But then Salem figured something out.

"I'm going to lean back and try to pull the front of the sled up just a little," he said. "Everyone lean back a little with me." Quickly, that's what he did.

We started to pick up speed. The wind whipped our faces. And then we really began to move. You could feel every bump in the road, and there seemed to be a lot of them. I could hear Salem shouting "Wheee!" at the front. London wasn't saying a word right in front of me. Georgia was quiet behind me, too, but still patting me on the back.

The metal sheet worked amazingly well as a sled. It never skidded off into a ditch. I never had to put my feet down. We built up just enough speed to go down that entire hill at medium rollercoaster speed – straight and fast, a whole lot faster than we could have walked the same distance.

Our sled coasted to a stop at the bottom of the hill, in a clearing where there weren't nearly as many pine trees. We all sat there for a second, breathless and still excited from the ride.

Georgia broke the silence. "Again!" she said.

"She's never said that before," Salem said delightedly. "She's learned a new word!"

"That's great, Georgia," I said, happy about the ride myself. It had been great. For a moment, I had forgotten that Mom and Dad were trapped in our van somewhere, hurt and bleeding, and that we were trying to save them. "Georgia, can you say 'again' again?"

But before she said anything, London had climbed off the sled. He stared off to the right side of the road through the snow, pointing.

"Look," he said. "Over there!"

It was a bear cub – jet black, with a brown muzzle.
It seemed to be almost exactly the size of London. It
was on all fours, its ears pricked up.

And it was walking right toward us.

CHAPTER 7

THE BEARS

We all stared in silence at the bear cub walking through the snow. It wasn't in any hurry — it kept lifting its snout to sniff the air. It was still about 30 yards away from us.

"Prippy!" Georgia said. That was the way she said "pretty."

"What kind is it?" Salem asked in a whisper.

"It has to be a black bear," I said. "We studied them in school. They're about the only kind of bears left in North Carolina."

"I thought bears all hibernated in the winter," Salem said.

"Maybe it's looking for its Christmas presents," London said. You could tell he was very happy about the bear, and also liked the fact he had spotted it first.

"We read about that," I said. "Up north, where it snows all the time, they can hibernate for five or six months. But in North Carolina, because they can find food almost all the time, they don't hibernate nearly as long. Some of them don't even hibernate at all."

The cub suddenly plopped down beside a bush that had some red berries on it and started eating them.

"Can we get closer?" London asked. "I want to see what it's eating. Do you think we can keep it for a pet, Chapel?"

"No, that's not a good idea," I said. "Whenever you see a bear cub, you can bet the mother is around."

But the bear cub almost seemed to hear London's wish to get a better look. I think it was curious about us, too. It got back on all fours and walked a slow half-circle around us, getting a little closer with every step. Then it stopped again, this time directly on the road in front of us, only about 20 yards away now. Then it just stared at us. I could see the cub's soft brown eyes.

"Kitty?" Georgia asked from behind me. She thought most animals were kitties.

"No, Georgia, not a kitty," Salem said softly.

As I looked at the bear, I remembered what I had seen on that pine tree beside our homemade sled. Those parallel lines must have been claw marks – a bear marking its territory. And the woolly worms? Those had probably been bits of bear fur. I had seen on TV on a nature show once about how bears would back up to a tree and scratch themselves in places their paws couldn't reach. It had seemed funny then. Not now. Those little fur balls had been way, way too high for this cub's back to have made them.

"OK," I said, my voice low. "That cub is in our way. We've got to keep going down this road. But I bet if we start walking toward it, the bear will run off. Black bears are supposed to be shy."

Then Salem got one of his ideas – the kind you can't talk him out of because he acts on them so quickly. He's not just our family athlete. Mom says he is our family extremist.

"If we can't keep him as a pet, then I'm going to scare him off for us," Salem said. "He's not any bigger than me."

And before I could stop him, he started running directly at the bear cub, his hands held high in the air, yelling: "Roar! Roar!"

"Salem!" I yelled.

"Kitty!" Georgia yelled.

But he didn't hear either one of our screams, because just then the bear cub let out a yowl. It sounded amazingly human, like the way Georgia cries when she's upset. If she wasn't still in the backpack, calling a cub a kitty, I would have thought it was her.

The bear backed up a few steps, but not very far. Salem tried to skid to a stop a few feet before he got to the bear, but for once his athletic ability let him down. Instead of stopping gracefully like he always did on the soccer field, he slipped on the snow and fell.

We all watched Salem tumble down about 10 feet from the bear cub, and we were studying the two of them so closely that it took us a few seconds before we saw what happened next.

Coming out of the woods, obviously alerted by her cub's cry for help, was a much larger black bear.

While the bear cub was cute, the big bear was not. It was enormous. And scary. The mother bear was bigger than my dad, and he's 6-feet-2 and weighs 200 pounds. She was black, too, like her cub, but she had a white patch on her chest that the cub didn't have. The mother bear was walking fast on all fours, and you could see her teeth. She was making a loud noise that sounded like the "Woof, woof!" of a large dog. This was a strange bear family, I thought in the midst of my terror. The cub sounds like a baby, and the mother sounds like a dog.

It took the mother bear only a few seconds to catch up to her cub. She got right beside the cub, which nuzzled its way back under her front legs until it was almost completely hidden. The mother bear was now only 10 feet away between her cub and Salem.

"Run away, Salem!" I said. "Run!"

I was more scared than I've ever been. I didn't want to get Georgia anywhere near a huge bear, and it took too long to get the backpack off. But I needed Salem to get away from there fast. I didn't know what to do.

But Salem didn't go anywhere. Still on the ground in his snowsuit, he looked up at the bears. I didn't know if he was paralyzed by fright or just curious, but I couldn't wait any longer. I looked around the side of the road for some sort of weapon that maybe could scare the bears away.

And then I saw London. he had found a pine tree branch at least as tall as he was. He was holding it straight out like a sword. And he was charging – charging! – right at the bears.

"Go away!" London yelled. The hood of his snowsuit flew off his head because he was running so fast. His red hair trailed behind him like a flame. "Leave my brother alone!"

If London was running toward the bears, I figured I better be his backup. I thought maybe throwing something wouldn't be a bad idea. The snow was deep and wet enough now that you could make a decent snowball. So I scooped two handfuls up while running a few feet behind London.

The mother bear saw us coming. She lifted off all fours for a second and stood up to her full height, glaring at us. Her ears were laid back onto her skull. She opened her mouth wide and this time, instead of a woof, let out a tremendous "ROOOOOAAAR!!!!"

But London didn't stop. He just kept running at the bears and screaming. "Go away! Go away!"

The mother bear lifted her right paw and swung it at London's pine tree branch. The blow connected and knocked the smallest third of the branch off the top, splitting the branch so you could see the white wood underneath.

London didn't stop, though, and with his home-made sword he hit the bear right in the white patch on her chest. It wasn't a hard shot, but the bear did look surprised before she batted the stick away and roared once more. London backed away a couple of steps when she did that, and so did I. Salem just kept sitting there.

But you know what?

London's charge actually worked.

The mother bear seemed to think about it for a second or two. Then she turned toward the woods, and so did her cub. They started jogging away – not very fast, but definitely running.

"Yeah, run!" I said. "Run!" I happily threw my snowball at them as they retreated, remembering to rear back and lead with my left foot like I was throwing a baseball.

The snowball toss was maybe the best throw I had ever made – it hit the mother bear right on her back. That seemed to make her run a little faster, with her bear cub right behind her. A few flakes of snow actually stuck to the bear's fur where I had hit her. When the two bears got to the nearest good-sized pine tree, the bear cub started climbing it. Then, right behind the cub, there went the mother. They climbed about 15 feet, then rested on a couple of branches and stared solemnly back at us.

My heart felt like it was about to burst. I was so proud of London – and a little proud of myself, too, for my snowball throw.

"London!" I said. "You ran those bears up the tree! I thought you were scared of bears."

"I am," he said, looking at the ground and shrugging his shoulders. "Well... I was."

Salem got up finally, and then hugged London. He had sat there and watched the whole thing. "You did it, London!" he said. "I can't believe it! Thank you!"

"That's the bravest thing I've ever seen anybody do," I said, and honestly, it made me look at London in a way I hadn't before. He wasn't just a 5-year-old little brother who didn't have to go to school and liked to get out of our nightly cleanup work by saying he was tired. He had been brave, the way knights were when they had to go fight a dragon.

"Londy, Londy!" Georgia said.

London didn't say anything else. He got this funny look he gets when he's trying not to smile, with the corners of his mouth turned down and his chin all wrinkled up. I do the same thing sometimes, Mom says. It's like our face doesn't want to admit we want to smile.

"That was great, London," I said again. "But we've got to get going. The bears are gone. Let's keep going straight down the road. At some point there's got to be a car, or a house, or something."

CHAPTER 8

THE DARK

I don't know how we walked as far as we did that night. It got colder and darker, but the snow finally stopped and the moon came out. That helped. We could see the road better then. We kept thinking that someone might drive by, but no one ever did. I guess our body heat from walking so much made us warm, because inside my snowsuit I didn't feel cold at all. Georgia was good about keeping the hood of her snowsuit on and zipped all the way up – you could see her eyes and her nose under that white hood and the blue helmet she was still wearing under it, but that was all.

But oh my gosh, she was getting heavy. She went to sleep for awhile while I was lugging her around – she had missed her regular nap – and I kept getting Salem to look back there for me to make sure she seemed OK. She woke up after about an hour, and then I got Salem to give her another bank sucker to keep her happy.

London was getting tired, too. After he ran off the bear, he almost had seemed to be floating down the road for the next hour. You could tell he was proud of himself, and we were proud of him, too. But his legs weren't as long as ours and, even though Salem had his backpack and I had Georgia, he was the one who asked for water breaks the most. We were going to run out of water before too long, but that wouldn't make our list of Top 10 problems. We could always eat snow if we had to.

I looked at my watch again at 9 p.m. I could see the watch's hands by the moonlight. We had been walking for most of the past five hours. Even with breaks for water and the few minutes we had spent chasing off the bear, and the fact we had definitely slowed down some in the last couple of hours, we had to have covered at least seven miles. Maybe eight.

And we hadn't seen a soul. Not a car. Not a person. Not a house. Nothing. I thought the world was supposed to be so crowded — there were six billion people in it, our teacher had said in social studies class — but it seemed deserted to us. We had yelled "Help!" every time we made it to the top of another hill at first. But lately, we hadn't even been trying that. It made us feel too lonely every time nobody answered.

"Are we going to walk all night, Chapel?" Salem asked. His teeth chattered a little as he said it, and I felt a sudden burst of sympathy for him. He had been carrying all our water and snacks, which hadn't run out yet because we had stocked up so thoroughly at that gas station. But that sort of load couldn't be easy for a second-grader. Neither could walking for this long.

"Not all night," I said. "I don't think any of us could do that. But I don't know where to stop. We've got to stay warm tonight. And we've got to find help somehow."

"I'm tired," London said. His voice sounded the way it does when he is nearly asleep. I know the voice, because the three of us share a single room at home. We've got two mattresses on the floor, and I always have to sleep nearest the closet because the other two are scared of what might be in there.

My body was aching, too. I had never walked even one mile before with Georgia on the backpack, I was sure. She weighed 22 pounds — I remember that from the last time we put her on the scale. And now I had walked seven or eight of them.

"Well, I'm tired, too," I snapped. "But I don't see any hotels out here. Do you?" I was sorry right after I said that, but I was tired of being the one who had to break the bad news. Didn't they understand? Why did I always have to be the leader? "If we're going to sleep for awhile, we're going to have to find a place that's sheltered. We won't be able to keep Georgia warm enough otherwise."

"It's OK," Salem said to me, and I could tell he was trying to calm me down. "We can walk all night if you want to, Chapel. We may just have to go slower."

I thought about it. "Let's go a little longer," I said, "at least to the top of the next hill. We'll take a look from there."

That we had a destination in mind gave Salem a sudden spurt of energy. "Carry my backpack for a minute, Chapel," he said. "I'll run up there to the top and see if there's anything good to see."

I didn't try to stop him. I took the backpack and held it in my gloved hand as he sprinted the last 50 yards to the top of the hill. Then he waved his arms frantically, motioning for us to come toward him.

"C'mon!" he said. "There's a house down there!"

CHAPTER 9

THE HOUSE

That made us all start running. We forgot about how tired we were and ran up the hill toward Salem. Georgia squealed in delight on my back and patted me, saying, "Go, go, go!"

We got to the top of the hill and looked down where Salem was pointing. It was a mobile home, surrounded by pine trees on three sides. There were no cars that I could see. There were no lights on. But it was something – the first real sign of life we had seen.

"Run down there and knock on the door," I told Salem. "Take your backpack this time. I'll get the little ones down there in a couple of minutes. Tell whoever answers that we need help and to call 9-1-1."

He sped down the hill toward the house, which was pretty close to the road. "C'mon now, London," I said. "Be careful on this hill."

But London wasn't moving. He had dropped to his knees, and now he lay down on his stomach in the middle of the road. "I'm staying here," he said sleepily. "I'm going to sleep right here. It's good." He shifted his head so that his hood blocked the snow from his face and acted like a small pillow.

"You can't, London!" I said. "We're so close!"

But he wouldn't budge. He lay on his stomach and closed his eyes and, even when I pushed him with my foot, he just grunted a little and kept his eyes closed. He was completely exhausted.

I knew I had to get him off the road and out of the cold. But I didn't know if I could. I was so tired. I got behind him, bent down and grabbed him under both shoulders.

"Mmmmph," he said.

"Shh, shh," I said. "Don't worry. I gotcha." It was what Dad told him at night when London fell asleep on the couch and had to be carried to our room. I had heard him say it many times before. London relaxed in my arms when he heard it.

I started to drag him down the hill, which wasn't easy with the way his tennis shoes kept sticking on stuff and with Georgia still on my back. But knowing that mobile home was there must have given me some extra strength. I was somehow able to manage both of them. I had dragged London all the way to the mobile home's front door in a couple of minutes.

But where was Salem?

"Salem!" I yelled. "Salem!"

Georgia was behind me and started saying softly: "She-she. She-she." That was the way she always said Salem's name.

He came running around the corner, a little out of breath.

"I knocked and knocked," he said, "and I yelled some, too. But no one's there. All the doors are locked. There's graffiti painted on the wall around the back, though – do you think gangsters live here?"

"I don't know," I said slowly. We always liked to talk about gangsters – that's how we described all bad guys. Could some of them live here but just be gone right now, out committing crimes until it was their bedtime?

I decided we had to get inside that mobile home, no matter who lived in there. There might be a phone. And even if there wasn't, it'd be a lot warmer than where we were.

"Can you find a way in, Salem?" I asked, knowing this was the type of job he would love. "You're probably the only one of us who could do that."

He nodded. "There's a window on the side that looks like I might be able to crawl into," he said. "I'll try to do that and then let you in the front door."

He must have done it, because it wasn't 30 seconds before he was opening the front door. I could hear the lock unlatch and then saw the door creak open.

"Surprise!" Salem said happily.

London, who I still had hold of under his shoulders, didn't stir. "Help me get London and Georgia in there," I told Salem. "Then we'll look for a phone."

We dragged London through the front door and then let him plop down in the hallway on his back, using the hood of his jacket as a pillow. Then I got Georgia off my back, as Salem helped me unload the backpack and then unlatch her. We took her helmet off, too. We had gotten her to walk around a couple of times during the water breaks, but mostly she had been up there for five hours. When I put her on her feet, she immediately sat down on her bottom and pointed at her legs.

"Hurt," she said.

"Oh, your legs probably went to sleep," I said. "Salem, rub her legs for a minute. I'm going to look for a phone."

The mobile home was small, with just four rooms – a kitchen, a bedroom, a bathroom and a den. It didn't look like anyone had lived there for a long time. There were a few empty beer bottles and an old McDonald's bag on the floor in the den. But there was no furniture and no carpet. There was a lot of dust. I found what looked like animal droppings in the kitchen. When I pushed open the bathroom door, a startled mouse ran into a hole in the wall. There was no phone I could see and no electricity – I turned on every light switch I could find, but nothing worked. I could see a little because of the moonlight streaming in the window Salem had gone through and the door we had left open.

I walked back into the hallway, where London was sound asleep and Salem was still rubbing Georgia's legs.

"Are you OK, Georgia?" I asked.

"Kay," she said. She stood up and walked a few steps to me, holding her arms out for me to pick her up. I did.

"It doesn't look like there's much of anything here, but I think we should sleep awhile," I said. "Mom and Dad would want us to do that. We'll keep going in the morning."

Salem thought about it. "Do you think you or me should just go on alone?" he said. "The other one could stay with London and Georgia here, and one of us could keep going down the road. Maybe we'd find help faster. I could do it if you want me to."

It wasn't a bad idea, I had to admit. Then I thought about what Mom had told me when we left her and Dad pinned in the van. Mom had said then: "No matter what you do, stay together."

"It could work," I told Salem. "But Mom really wanted us to stay together. Whoever went could get lost or get frostbite or something."

"OK," Salem said. "But we're already lost, aren't we?" He didn't argue, though. Salem was exhausted, too. He arranged his backpack near London's head as a pillow and curled up next to him. Since London was a little big for his age and Salem a little small for his, they were almost the same size. They looked like two puppies, snuggling into each other for warmth.

A few moments passed in silence. The moonlight cast shadows inside the mobile home.

"Chapel?" Salem asked, and I could tell he was half-asleep already. "Do we need to brush our teeth?"

"It's OK," I said. "Not tonight."

"Are we going to find somebody in time to help Mom and Dad?" he asked. He sounded like he was about to cry.

"We are," I said, as firmly as I could. I said a prayer then for us, and for Mom and Dad. Even though I whispered most of it, Salem said "Amen" at the end. Georgia was sitting in my lap by then, her eyes drooping. I gave her a couple of sips from our last bottled water, and she fell asleep on my chest. I leaned up against the wall. I thought about staying up all night, trying to think of a better plan, but I guess I didn't. The fawn with the white spots flashed into my mind again – I don't know why. It felt like I just closed my eyes for a minute.

And then, suddenly, I was getting shaken awake.

CHAPTER 10

THE MORNING

"Chapel! Chapel! Wake up!" Salem said. "We have to get going."

I didn't know where I was for a minute. I thought it was a school day, and Dad was downstairs fixing my cheese grits and Salem's oatmeal, and maybe I was a few minutes late waking up. Maybe the heat in our house was off, too – because I was freezing.

Then it all came flooding back. The wreck. The snow. The sled. The bears. The walk. And now this old abandoned mobile home. I pushed the "light" button on my watch. It said 4:30 a.m. I had never been a morning person.

"Too early," I mumbled.

"No, we have to go now!" Salem said. "Mom and Dad are waiting for us to get help!"

He was right. I usually like to start my mornings with a half-cup of coffee out of my parents' coffee-pot – they are totally addicted to the stuff and they think it's OK for me to drink it, too. But we didn't have anything left except for a small bag of Crunchy Cheetos, half of a bottle of water and one small bag of M&Ms.

"OK," I said. "Let me use the bathroom."

I walked outside to do that, because I hadn't liked the looks of that mouse in the mobile home's bath-room last night. When I walked outside, it was still cold, but it didn't feel quite as bad as it had been the night before when we stopped. I came back inside, feeling a little bit better.

"Do you know what day it is?" I asked Salem. He shook his head.

"It's Christmas," I said. "Christmas morning."

That phrase made London stir. "Christmas?" he said, sitting up on the floor but still half-asleep. "Where are the presents?"

Salem and I both glanced around. We knew in our hearts there weren't going to be any presents inside this mobile home, which was fairly disgusting but had also done us a big favor as our shelter for the night. And yet the whole situation was so unreal, so weird, that we both took a look, as if a Christmas tree with gifts might have just materialized out of the air.

There was nothing, of course. It was still dark outside, but we could see a little inside the mobile home because of the moonlight.

"There aren't any presents, London," I said. "Not here. We'll have to have Christmas once we get back with Mom and Dad."

Mom and Dad. How were they doing? I hoped so much a car had come by, followed our van's tracks, found our parents and taken them to the hospital. But I doubted it. Any car that found them would have had to circle around the barrier my dad did. And if it had come from the way we were walking, we would have seen it. I tried not to think about the fact that it was going to be hard to find the van, too, because the tire tracks from yesterday would now be covered by fresh snow.

"It's a white Christmas," Salem said, pulling his backpack back on. "We've never had a white Christmas before."

"No, we haven't," I said. "And we're never going to forget this one either. One day, we're going to think back about this day and think all of it is funny."

"I don't think it's funny," London said.

"Not right now," I said. "What I mean is…."

But I didn't finish that thought, because then right beside me was a wail. "Maaaa-maaaa!" Georgia said. "Nurse!"

Georgia was used to sleeping beside Mom at night. She still nursed. All of us had nursed until we were two years old at least, although I don't go around telling any of my friends about that nowadays.

We started scrambling around trying to make Georgia happy. Salem took off his backpack and started talking to her in his sweetest voice about how Mom wasn't here right now but we'd see her before too long. London got a fresh diaper out for her. And I dug through Salem's backpack, got the one pack of M&Ms we had left and tore it open.

"How about M&Ms for breakfast?" I asked Georgia.

She looked at it. "Can-dee," she said.

"That's right," I said. "Go ahead and eat it. We're just all going to need a good teeth-brushing later." Ugh – that sounded just like something Dad would say.

London changed Georgia's diaper again – she held still because she had a couple of M&Ms to keep her happy. No one even asked her to share the candy. That never would have happened two days ago, when one kid getting a single M&M more than another seemed like a national emergency to all of us.

But Georgia shared anyway, putting several M&Ms in both London and Salem's mouth and then laughing happily when they crunched them up. By 4:45 a.m., we were back on the road, cold but determined. We split the Cheetos while we walked. That meant we didn't have any more food at all, but I tried not to think about that.

CHAPTER 11

THE KITCHEN COUNTER

We walked for three hours straight that morning. We walked as the sunrise slowly lit a path for us. I'm sure it was beautiful, but we hardly noticed it. It was cold and we were hungry. But we kept walking. About an hour into our walk, we realized we had left Georgia's helmet behind at the mobile home, but it was too late by then to go back. To pass the time – and to keep our minds off the fact that it had now been about 16 hours since we had left Mom and Dad at the van – we started telling stories about things that had happened to our family.

We talked about other Christmases and the presents we had gotten and the parts we had played in the Salem Methodist Church Christmas play. Usually you could count on at least two of us being wise men each year, and on none of us being too hot about being the wise man who had to hold the myrrh. We talked about our pet tree frog we had once, which we had named "Mojo Stickypants." We talked about the two pet lizards we had one time. We talked about our dog Ringo, who was at home with our neighbors but who would have loved all this walking in the woods, except the part with the bears. He would have been terrified about that. We talked about our cousins – Davis, Jackson, Banks, Sawyer, Kyler, Korbin, Tristan, Paige, Brittany, Jason, Ellis, Eden, Brennan, Levi, Ronnie and all the rest of them. We had a lot of cousins.

And we talked about our dreams.

"Remember that time you had that dream, Chapel?" Salem said. "It was your 10th birthday party?"

"Oh, yeah," I said. "For some reason it was at a roller-skating rink, and every girl in fourth and fifth grades came. And not a single boy. It was horrible."

When we got thirsty, we would scrape some snow off of a tree limb or a bush and eat that. London made himself a snowball and carried it in his gloves for awhile, munching on it.

"This is my snowcone," London said.

"What flavor is it then?" Salem said, a challenge in his voice.

"Plain," London said.

That was such a good answer that Salem decided to make himself one, too.

We all started talking about food after awhile. It was hard not to because we were all so hungry. We talked about the diner we loved to go with Mom and Dad on Saturday mornings, where we got scrambled eggs and bacon and pancakes piled high and served with all the butter and syrup you want. Mom would usually get a vegetable omelet instead of all that stuff, which was crazy. She'd always want asparagus in the omelet, which London still called "despair-agus." Given how it tasted, I thought that was a good nickname.

"Remember that time you were in a hurry to wash your hands at the diner and get back to the table because you knew the food was coming?" I asked Salem.

"Oh yeah," he said. "Dad asked me if I washed my hands and I said, 'I washed one of them.'"

We went on like that for awhile. I told them the story of what I had said when I was five, Salem was two and Mom and Dad had asked me what I thought about getting another baby.

I had started crying. "What's wrong?" Mom said.

I had pointed at Salem and moaned: "But I don't want to take this one back!"

It wasn't the kind of story I usually told – too sappy – but it was Christmas after all.

All of us can remember all kinds of stuff – tiny details that our parents always say they've forgotten about things that happened to us. Mom says that's because our brains aren't all filled up yet with boring stuff like grocery lists and which bill needs to be paid next.

"Remember that joke you made up about the kitchen, London?" I asked. I was still trying to be nice, and he looked like he might be getting tired again.

"Yes," London said, brightening at the thought. "I'm going to tell it again. What does the kitchen counter say?"

"I don't know," I said, and when Salem started to say something, I gave him a warning look. "What does it say?"

"It says '1-2-3,'" London said. "Get it, Chapel? The kitchen counter counts!"

"I get it," I said.

"OK," London said. "Now I'm going to tell it again…."

And he did tell it again. And again. And even once more after that, enough times that Georgia was able to say, "One-two-free" the last time he asked the question.

"That's right, Georgia," Salem said as we reached the top of another small hill. "You counted to three!"

And then we all looked down and were totally speechless for a second. There was a small house directly below us, with a short driveway. There were lights on in the windows. And there was smoke rising out of the chimney.

CHAPTER 12

THE OLD LADY

This time we didn't send Salem down first. We all ran together as fast as we could – up the driveway, then down a short sidewalk and then up two steps to the front door. The door had a Christmas bow on it just above the door knocker. There was a small lighted reindeer in the front yard, and the lights were on. Salem arrived first and started banging on the knocker. London, Georgia and I got there a couple of seconds later. I saw a doorbell, lit by a pale orange glow, and pressed that once.

"I want to press it, too!" London said. He always liked to press elevator buttons, too.

"OK," I said happily. "It won't hurt anything."

Somebody lived here. That was obvious. I felt like we were a few seconds away from getting help for Mom and Dad. Georgia felt as light as a feather on my back.

But no one came to the door. No dog barked. Salem knocked again. London rang the doorbell again. Still, we didn't hear anything.

"Ope," Georgia said. That's how she said "open."

"Good idea, Georgia," I said. "Let's try."

I reached for the doorknob and turned. It wasn't locked. I gave the door a small push and it opened with a lingering creak. Even from the doorstep, the house felt warm.

"Hello?" I said. And then, a little louder, as I stepped through the door into a small hallway: "Hello?! Excuse me? We need help!"

The boys followed right behind me as I took a few more steps inside. It was so hot. It was like the warmth was inviting us inside, even though nobody else was. I thought I smelled coffee.

I looked behind me and saw everybody was inside. "Shut the door," I whispered to Salem. "We shouldn't let the cold air in."

I was about to say "Hello" again when Georgia beat me to it. She had something different on her mind, however.

"Ma-ma??" she said. "Ma-ma?"

And this time... this time, we heard a reply.

"Who's there?" someone said. "Did you forget something, Arthur?"

The voice sounded like it belonged to an old woman. It came from down the hall. Maybe she hadn't heard us the first time. Maybe she was hard of hearing.

I looked at London and Salem. They looked at me, wide-eyed and mute. I knew I was going to have to handle this one.

"Umm, no ma'am," I said. "It's not Arthur. It's...."

"Come in here, child," the voice said. "I can't hear you."

And so we did. We shuffled down the hallway, single file. I don't know why we felt scared after all we had been through, but we were. We had time to see framed pictures on the hallway wall – old family photos, I thought. There was a man, a woman and a boy in most of them – the child first as a baby, then as a kid about my age, then as someone much older than me.

It was 10 steps down the hallway until we entered the room where the voice had come from. We walked into the room one at a time until we were all standing there, silently.

There was a couch with two multi-colored afghan blankets on it. The walls were wood paneling.

There was an ancient TV in the corner. There was a small fire in the fireplace and a Christmas wreath hanging above it.

There was also one rocking chair, and in that chair sat the oldest woman I had ever seen. She was a black woman, and there were so many lines in her face it was hard to see where the wrinkles stopped and her eyes began. She was tiny. I'm five feet tall and weigh 95 pounds, and I think I may have been a little bigger than she was.

The old woman had glasses perched on her nose and what looked like a cup of coffee beside her on a small red table. I could see two cups sitting on the table – one was half-full, the other completely empty. The table also held a lamp and a Bible, which was open and had print so large I could make out what chapter she was reading from where I was. She had been reading Luke, which made sense because it told the most famous version of the story of Jesus's birth. I knew that from Sunday School and from what Linus says in that old Charlie Brown Christmas special that still comes on every year, the one that always makes my Mom sad because the other kids are so mean about the tree Charlie Brown picked out.

The old lady wore a faded dress and purple house shoes, the kind you can slip on and off without bending down.

Georgia, maybe sensing our nervousness, started to whine a little. I don't think the old lady could see too well, because it didn't seem like she had noticed Georgia in the backpack behind me until she heard that noise.

"Oh, Lord," she said to me. "Is that a baby on your back?"

"Yes, ma'am," I said, and then the words started tumbling out of me like a waterfall. "We had a wreck and we need a phone and our parents are trapped and we've been walking so long and..."

"Hold on, child," she said, raising one hand. "Hold on. These ears don't work so good anymore. Slow down. But before you do anything else, bring me that baby."

I hesitated. I loved Georgia more than anything else in the world. Surely this old lady didn't mean to harm her, did she?

I decided to bring Georgia to her but then stand beside her while she held Georgia. It might get us going faster.

Salem helped me unstrap Georgia from the backpack. Then I held her on my hip and walked across the room to the ancient lady. Normally, Georgia doesn't go to any stranger without a fight – instead, she will lean her head back down onto the shoulder of the person she's familiar with.

This time, though, Georgia put out her arms and let the black lady take her. When Georgia settled onto the lady's lap, looking intently at the pattern on her dress, the lady beamed with delight. Georgia often has that sort of effect on people.

"Oh, if you aren't the sweetest thing," the lady said. "I've been waiting so long to meet you."

That sounded weird. To meet her?

"Her name is Georgia," I said. "Can we use your phone? We have to call 911, right away. Our parents are hurt, and we've been walking forever."

"Oh, honey!" she said, smiling even more broadly. "Her name is Georgia? That's my name, too. Georgia Abigail Swann. Most people just call me Miss Swann."

"OK," I said, figuring I could save the talk about strange coincidences for after the ambulance was called. "Miss Swann, can you tell me where the phone is?"

"Oh, honey," she said, jiggling Georgia gently on her knee. "I don't have a phone."

My heart sank. She didn't have a phone. How could a lady who had to be about 200 years old live way out here with no phone?

"Even a cell phone?" I asked, knowing the answer but asking anyway.

"A what?" Miss Swann said.

"Who takes care of you?" asked Salem. He and London had moved close to the fire and were standing there with their backs to it.

"Oh, that would be Arthur," she said. "My son."

"Is he here?" Salem asked.

"No, honey," Miss Swann said. "I live here all alone. I like it by myself. But Arthur comes and checks on me every day at 6:30 a.m. Drives all the way out here from town, then drives right back in to go to work at the Mini Mart. He built that fire this morning. He made this coffee. You didn't miss him by much. But the Mini Mart is the only store open around here on Christmas Day. He just left."

He just left. The words rattled hollowly around in my head. What if we had started 15 minutes earlier this morning? That must have been Arthur's coffee cup – the other one on the table. Couldn't he have stayed just a little longer?

"How far is town?" London said. He had been paying attention to the conversation, too.

"Oh, not that far," Miss Swann said. "Not more than five miles to the center of it. When I used to be able to drive, it took me no more than 10 minutes to get there."

Five miles. What was that? Another two hours of walking, at least? I pride myself on never crying, but suddenly my throat felt tight. I felt tears start to well up in my eyes. I had thought this was it, that this house was going to be the beginning of our rescue. And now we were still five miles away.

"How old are you, son?" Miss Swann said, peering at me through her eyeglasses.

"Eleven," I said.

"I don't reckon," she said, "that you know how to drive a truck?"

CHAPTER 13

THE TRUCK

My heart thudded in my chest. Me, drive a truck? I had never driven anything except a bicycle and a scooter.

"Eleven years old," Miss Swann said, stroking Georgia's hair lightly but looking at me. "You're probably a little too young. You may be a little short for it, too. Arthur's got the seat adjusted for him – he's six feet, four inches tall – and it won't rise up for short people anymore, I believe. But you can try it if you want."

"Can't you drive us?" I asked.

"Oh no, honey," Miss Swann said. "I haven't driven for 10 years – I gave up my license when I was 75 years old. I can barely see anymore unless you're right up in front of me."

"But you have a truck?" Salem asked.

"Yes," Miss Swann said, tilting her head in Salem's direction. "Never did get rid of it. It's out back under the carport. Arthur uses it sometimes when his own car is in the shop."

She paused for a second. "Now, wait a minute – how old are you?" she said to Salem. "And tell me all your names."

"I'm Salem," he said, rocking from one foot to another, "and I'm eight. Chapel is the big brother. I'm the middle brother. This red-headed kid is London. He's five. And you know Georgia – she's 19 months old."

"Oh, yes," the woman said, rocking. "I know Georgia. I've been waiting for Georgia."

There she went again. Miss Swann sounded a little strange, but then again, she was 85. More importantly, she had a truck. We told her quickly about our accident and what we had done since then. She nodded without speaking, taking it all in. When we quickly went through the part about the bears, she smiled at London and said, "Now you're a brave little thing, aren't you?"

After we finished the short version of the story, I asked: "Where are the keys to your truck?"

"They're on the TV," Miss Swann said. "So your name is Chapel? Like a church?"

"Yes," I said. "Like a church."

"OK, Chapel," she said. "I think I know how you might be able to drive the truck – with some help. Here. Take your sister back for a minute and follow me. We're all going to go with you."

I took Georgia back from Miss Swann, and she slowly rose out of her rocking chair. Then she slowly took a cane I hadn't noticed – it had been leaning on the back of her chair. Then she slowly walked toward the hall. She did everything so slowly. I tried not to be impatient, but it was hard. I grabbed the keys off the top of the TV and motioned to the others to follow her.

We put on our coats again and zipped them as we walked behind Miss Swann out a back door. That back door had another sidewalk that led to the carport. The carport pointed straight out toward the road we had been walking on for so long. Underneath the carport was a dark blue truck, facing out toward the driveway. I took that as a good sign – at least I wouldn't have to back up.

Miss Swann stopped a few feet from the truck. "I'm going to catch my breath," she said. "The little boy, Georgia and I are going to ride in the back. You and your brother – Salem, that's right, isn't it? You two can get up front."

We walked in front of her, opened the truck door and started climbing in. I gave London a boost to get him into the back seat and Salem easily vaulted into the passenger seat. Then I lifted Georgia up to London to hold – "Londy, Londy!" she said joyfully. Miss Swann caught up after a few moments, and I put an arm under her elbow to help boost her up, too. She got right behind the driver's seat, breathing hard.

"OK," she said. "Now you climb in, Chapel, but don't put the key in yet."

I did as she said and sat in the driver's seat. And I realized quickly this wasn't going to work. I could barely see over the top of the steering wheel. I saw the sky fine, but I wasn't going to see the road at all.

"Can you see the hood of the car?" Miss Swann said.

"No ma'am," I said.

"I didn't think so," Miss Swann said. "Here. Sit on this."

From underneath the driver's seat, she dug out an ancient quilt that smelled like old shoes. I took it from her and bunched it up under me. It raised me up enough so that I could see the hood if I sat up completely straight.

"That worked!" I said excitedly.

"Now can you reach the pedals with your right foot?" she said.

Uh-oh. I hadn't thought of that. I straightened my leg and pointed my toe as far as it would go, but still couldn't touch either of the two pedals on the floor. When I stretched a little harder, I did touch the pedal, but I slid off the quilt and banged the horn with my arm.

"Ho-o-o-onk!"

We all jumped.

"I can't reach the pedals!" I said, starting to get panicky. "What are we going to do?"

"Salem," said Miss Swann, "you're going to have to...."

But Salem had figured out what she was going to say. He was already climbing up into my lap. He pulled the quilt out from under me, threw it into the passenger seat, and sat on top of me.

"We're going to drive it together, Chapel," he said. "I'll do the top part. You do the bottom."

"Yes," said Miss Swann. "That's it. Chapel works the pedals. Salem steers the wheel."

"OK," I said. Normally, I would have asked more questions. But we had to get going. I knew how to turn the key, at least – I had seen my parents do that many times.

The engine roared to life. "Which pedal is which?" I shouted.

"The right one is gas," Miss Swann said. "The left is brake. Use your right foot for both – don't use your left foot at all."

"Go, Chapel, go!" Salem said. He had gripped the steering wheel tightly in both hands. I had to scoot down so far to reach the pedals that I couldn't see anything except the back of his head.

I pushed with my right foot. First, I barely touched the pedal at all. Then, because nothing happened, I pushed a little harder. Then even harder. Still, nothing.

"Nothing's happening!" I shouted.

"Oh, goodness," Miss Swann said. "I'm forgetting something."

"What about the stick thing coming out of the steering wheel?" London said from the backseat. "I think Mom and Dad use that somehow when they drive."

"OK," Salem said. He took his right hand off the steering wheel and yanked down on the stick thing.

My right foot was still mashing the gas pedal as hard as it could when Salem pulled down on the stick, and it was like uncaging a hungry tiger. The truck leaped forward out of the carport and up the driveway, startling all of us.

"Too fast!" Miss Swann yelled. Panicked, I took my foot off the gas and jammed it onto the other pedal – the brake. I guess I hit it a little too hard, as we stopped like he had run into a brick wall. Salem hit his head on the steering wheel.

"Owww!" he said. "What are you doing?"

"I don't know!" I said. "I don't know what to do!"

"It's OK, boys," Miss Swann said. "Now just go more gently with the pedals, Chapel. And Salem, there's going to be a right turn out of the driveway. Get ready for it."

I pushed the gas pedal – nice and easy this time. I saw Salem above me, his tongue poking out of the corner of his mouth, concentrating on making the turn. I felt the truck turn, turn, turn… and then there was a scraping noise on the passenger's side. I took my foot off the pedal.

"Did you hit something, honey?" Miss Swann said. "I can't see."

"He ran into some bushes," London announced. "Get Salem *immediately* in…."

"It's OK," Miss Swann interrupted. "Try to keep going. The truck doesn't matter, as long as we're OK."

"Kay, kay," Georgia babbled. She was happy to get another car ride.

"OK," I said. "I'm going to push the gas again. Tell me if you want to go any faster, but whatever you do, don't have a wreck. We can't afford another one of those."

Salem kept steering and I kept pushing the pedal. The scraping noise started again, then stopped as we got clear of the bush.

"We're on the road now," Salem said.

I rose up for a moment to see and sat beside him. We were on a slight downhill slope, so the truck coasted while I looked. The road appeared to be straight for the next little while. There was snow on both sides, but it had mostly melted on the road.

"All right," I said. "I'm going to go a little faster."

I scooted back down to work the pedals. Salem kept both hands on the steering wheel. London, Georgia and Miss Swann were quiet in the back seat as we worked together, easing the truck up the road.

"Not so fast, Chapel," Salem said. "There's a turn coming up."

I slowed the truck down when he told me to and popped up occasionally to check our progress. Together, we guided the truck up one hill and down the next. It was starting to be fun.

"You're doing good, boys," Miss Swann said. "Not much longer and we'll get to Clarksville — that's the closest town."

"How come you don't live there?" London said. "You're old."

I winced, but Miss Swann didn't seem to mind. "I did live in Clarksville for most of my life," she said. "But my husband and I liked to be by ourselves in the woods. We moved outside of town 20 years ago, when we retired, to the house you came to today."

"What happened to him?" London asked.

"Six years ago, Sam died," Miss Swann said. "We had been married 58 years. Now Arthur – he was our only child – he wants me to come live with him. But I like where I am. Maybe one day, yes. But not yet."

Salem and I kept on driving. We were getting the hang of it. And then we had this weird thing happen, the sort of stuff they say happens to twins when your brains appear to be connected by some invisible wire for a few seconds. We had the same thought at the same time and suddenly said together: "Let's switch!"

So we did. It turned out I couldn't sit on Salem's lap – his feet were too short to reach the pedals – but we got around that. Instead, I just got on my knees in the front seat – I could see fine that way – and Salem got all the way down on the floorboard, his back against the driver's seat, and mashed the gas and brake when I told him to with his right foot. He was very careful, and so was I. And for the first time since the wreck, I was glad we weren't seeing any other cars.

"This road doesn't lead much of anywhere anymore," Miss Swann said. "It used to be well-traveled. But then they put the new highway in, and the state just let it wither away. Now it doesn't even show up on most maps."

"Why not?" London said. "It's still a road."

"I guess because it's a road to nowhere, really," Miss Swann said. "It's blocked off on one side. Not a single other house on it. There used to be some people who lived in a mobile home not too far away – that sounds like where you spent last night – but they left five or six years ago. There are a lot of days I never hear a single car except for Arthur's. Even the deer hunters don't come out this far anymore. Why was your dad driving on it, anyway?"

"He knew about it from when he was a kid or something," I said. "He thought it was a shortcut."

After only a few more minutes, I could see that the pine trees were starting to thin out. "I see some-thing!" I said. "Keep pushing the gas, Salem – we're almost there."

We rounded a gentle curve and then I saw the first road sign of our journey. It was on the right side, with white letters on a metallic green background. It read: "Welcome to Clarksville. Pop. 847."

CHAPTER 14

THE RETURN

"We're coming into Clarksville," I said excitedly to Miss Swann. "Where should we stop?"

"Let me think," Miss Swann said. "We could go to Arthur's store, but that's kind of in the middle of town. We'll pass a number of things before that...."

London pointed out the window. "Look," he said. "Another kid!"

"I want to see!" Salem said from down below, where he was still in charge of the gas and brake. "I want to see!"

"OK," I said, feeling good after my turn after the wheel. "Let's switch back." He climbed back onto my lap and I started working the pedals again while he controlled the steering wheel.

Before I slumped down to press them, though, I got a good look at the kid. He looked to be about Salem's age. He was riding a red bicycle on the road by himself.

"I bet he got that bike for Christmas," Salem said.

Christmas. It was Christmas morning, wasn't it? I kept forgetting that. This didn't seem anything like Christmas. It was all too weird.

"Let's not stop," I suggested. "We need grown-ups for this, not kids. Grown-ups and ambulances and stuff."

So I sank back into the seat and stepped on the gas. Salem guided us slowly past the kid.

"He's stopping his bike and watching us," London said. "Now we're going past him."

I couldn't resist popping up again to take one more look. London and Georgia were both waving at the kid from the backseat, but he didn't notice them at all. Instead, the kid was staring at Salem holding onto the steering wheel as we went by. I thought I knew what the kid's look meant: "Man, all I got was a stupid red bicycle for Christmas! That kid's my age, and he got a truck!"

Miss Swann spoke up from the backseat. "I know where we should stop," she said. "We'll go to the volunteer fire department. It's on this road, on the left — one of the very first things you see when you get into the town."

Only about two minutes later, Salem said, "I see it. Slow us down, Chapel."

I let off the gas pedal and lifted my head back up as we coasted. The fire department was on the left. It looked like there were two fire trucks parked inside a big garage. There was a gravel parking lot right beside the fire department. A red truck was the only car in the whole lot. There was a big sign that said "Clarksville V.F.D."

"OK, turn in there," I said to Salem. I scooted back down and touched the brake a little with my foot. I could see Salem turning the wheel to the left and then heard the crunch of our tires rolling over the gravel.

"Stop, stop!" Salem said. "We're about to hit another truck!"

I slammed the brakes down and we all jolted forward. Salem immediately got off my lap and moved to the passenger seat, where he started trying to open the door to get out.

I let off the brakes, and suddenly we started to roll again. "How do you make it stop for good?" I asked Miss Swann, pressing the brakes with all my might.

"Oh, it's been so long since I've done this," she said. "Let me see…"

"The stick thing," London said. "It kept us stopped at the beginning. Push it back up!"

I reached up and tried to. At first, it wouldn't go anywhere, but when I jiggled it back and forth a little while pushing straight up, it did move. Then I heard a clicking sound and the truck seemed to rock in place for a second. I carefully took my foot off the brake and the truck didn't move anymore. We had barely missed hitting the red truck in the parking lot, ending up about six inches short of the truck's bumper.

"Everybody out!" I said, turning the key off just like I'd seen Mom and Dad do. "Let's go inside."

We started unloading. But it was a time-consuming process with an 85-year-old woman and a baby in our group now. So well before we even got inside, a man stepped out of the fire station and met us. He looked to be a little older than my Dad, maybe about 50. He was a little shorter than Dad and looked strong and stout, with a mustache and hair that were both jet black. He was wearing a heavy black coat that matched his hair and was looking at the tiny gap between our truck and his.

"Merry Christmas," he said. "And nice parking job."

His face looked like it was about to smile for a second, but then it decided to stay blank. "Who exactly was driving your truck, anyway?"

"We were," I said, pointing to myself and Salem. "But..."

"You were?" he interrupted, his eyes narrowing. "You think letting kids drive a truck is funny?" His eyes cut over toward Miss Swann.

"No sir," I said. "But we've got an emergency."

"What sort of emergency?" he said, moving a couple of steps closer to take a better look at us. "Is this woman hurt?"

"I'm just fine," Miss Swann said. "This is my truck. I let them drive it because their parents are hurt."

"Where are they?" the man said.

"You know the road that used to lead to Springfield before the new highway came in? Davis Church Road?" Miss Swann said.

"Yeah," said the man. "But that's blocked off now. There's a barricade 18 or 20 miles up the road. Nothing down Davis Church Road anymore but trees."

"I'm down that way," Miss Swann corrected. "The only house on the road — at least the only one anybody lives in."

I interrupted, worried we were losing time. "My dad used to live around here," I said. "He went around that barricade yesterday. He knew he wasn't supposed to, but he said it would be a shortcut. Then he had a wreck trying to miss hitting a deer. My Mom and Dad were pinned inside the car. They sent us to get help, but they're still down there trapped. They're still down there right now!"

The man started moving then. I wouldn't have thought he could move that fast. But suddenly he had a radio in his hand and he was calling out numbers and names so quickly I couldn't understand all he was saying. I heard the word "Dispatch" in there a few times, and it sounded like he told whoever was on the other end of that radio that the volunteers on call needed to be paged, including the rescue squad people.

"I know it's Christmas," the man said to whoever it was on the other end of that radio. "But I need 'em."

The rescue squad was apparently located in another small town 15 minutes further down the road — that's where the closest ambulance was — but they would have the proper "extrication equipment."

Then he said to us: "One of you needs to ride with me. Ma'am, do you know where this wrecked van is?"

"Oh, Lord, no," Miss Swann said. "I wasn't there. You'll need to take Chapel for that. We'll pray for you from right here."

"OK," the man said, and he started taking charge. "My name's Butch. All the rest of you go inside the firehouse. There's a couch in there, and a TV, and it's warm. Help yourself to whatever you can find to eat. There's not much, but there may be some leftover Christmas cookies or something. I'll get someone else in here soon as I can to keep you up to date."

Then he turned to me, his big black boots crunching on the parking lot gravel. "OK, Chapel," he said. "You're going to ride in the fire truck. And you're going to help me find your parents. We'll find them first so the rescue squad will have one less thing to worry about. C'mon!"

I followed Butch to the big fire truck on the right – he said the other one was a "tanker" that was just for hauling extra water. "This truck is 20 years old," he said, climbing inside and patting the dashboard proudly. "But it'll get us there."

I sat right beside him in the passenger seat. Mom and Dad never let me sit up front, but Butch didn't seem to mind. The fire department's see-through garage door opened automatically. Butch flipped some switches, turned a key and the truck zipped out, siren blaring. I glanced back and saw Salem holding the door that led inside the firehouse for Miss Swann, who was holding Georgia in her arms. Georgia was looking back at me, waving. I could see her lips mouthing the word "Bye-bye."

"You were lucky I was here," Butch said. "This is an all-volunteer fire department, and we don't always have someone in here on holidays. We just carry pagers. I had hidden some presents near the fire truck for my kids, though – they are always snooping around the house – and I'd stopped in to get them before we had Christmas dinner."

In the fire truck, I told Butch our story. He turned off the siren once we got on the deserted road and listened while he drove, although sometimes I had to stop talking because he kept getting back on the radio to talk to other people. I got the idea that a lot of people were going to be on Davis Church Road before long. The road to nowhere would be filled up.

Butch asked me about directions and distances a few times, and I guessed as best I could. He asked me if I thought my parents were warm enough and if we had left them anything to drink and whether either one of them could talk when we had gone. I felt proud when he said it sounded like we had done a good job trying to cover them up and putting the water nearby. But I could tell he was worried about finding the van. All I knew for sure was that it was going to be a few miles after we passed Miss Swann's house.

"OK, Chapel," he said just after we went by Miss Swann's house on our left. "You're really going to have to guide me from here."

I started to worry. What if I couldn't find the van? We were so close now! But there had been new snow since then that may have covered the tire tracks. It would be terrible if we just kept driving up and down this road, wasting precious time.

We went past the abandoned mobile home where he had spent the night a few minutes later. None of this seemed nearly as far apart as it had when we were walking it, one step at a time.

"It can't be much further than this, can it?" Butch said, slowing the truck down considerably. "You four couldn't have gone much longer – not with that baby and the 5-year-old."

"But we did," I insisted. "That's where we spent the night, but we walked almost five hours before we got there. I was guessing in my head it would be seven more miles."

Butch checked the thing on the car dashboard that tells you how many miles you've gone. "I don't think it could possibly be that long," he said. "But we'll know soon."

The next 10 minutes crawled by. We both kept turning our heads back and forth, trying to see down in the ditches on each side of the road. I knew the wreck had been on the right side when we had it – so that would be our left side now – but I could tell Butch didn't quite believe me on that. He kept swiveling his head from one side to the other, like the barn owl at the Raptor Center where we like to go to in Charlotte.

"I'm pretty sure it's still just a little further," I said.

"Son," Butch said, "I just don't think you could have walked that far. Now I'm sure it *felt* like you went that far, but we don't have time for wild goose chases. We've got to find your parents fast. I'm going to turn the truck around."

Then I freaked out a little. "No!" I said. "No! I know how far we went! I was out there! I know! Don't turn around yet! You've gotta keep going!"

Butch looked at me, considering things. "OK, son," he said. "We'll go a little more."

He kept the truck pointed straight. But everything looked exactly the same on both sides of the road. Snow and trees. Trees and snow. Over and over.

"I think it's time to backtrack now," Butch said after a few more minutes. He slowed down, preparing to put the truck into reverse. This time I wasn't sure I should argue.

And then I saw a flash of white and brown.

A fawn.

It was standing on the side of the road, staring at the truck. I saw the white spots, blending into the snow. Then, just as quickly, the fawn darted back off into the trees.

"Stop," I said. "This is it!"

"What?" Butch said, who was in the middle of turning the fire truck's big steering wheel. "Where?"

"I saw a fawn," I said. "I think it's a sign! It was probably the same baby deer we almost ran over! This may be where the fawn lives!"

"There are hundreds of deer in these woods, son," Butch said. "I can't imagine...."

But I didn't listen to the rest. I found the door handle, opened it and scrambled out of the fire truck before Butch could say anything. I knew he would follow me. I hadn't seen any sign of the van, but I had this feeling.... I just *knew* it was there. The fawn had reminded me of something. It was like the star the three wise men followed when they were looking for Jesus. The fawn felt like my own personal star.

"Hold up there, son!" Butch said, and I could tell he was irritated. "Chapel! We can't waste time!"

I was already running down the hill, though. I knew we were almost there. And then, I *really* knew. I saw the white bark of a small tree that had nearly been sawed in half. And then, just a few steps later, I saw our van – snow covering its roof, mostly hidden in the trees, but definitely our van.

"It's down here, Butch!" I said. "Hurry!"

I could hear him running behind me, but I didn't stop. I ran to the passenger side door, afraid of knowing what had happened to Mom and Dad but more afraid of not knowing. I leaped into the side door, where we had all been able to escape. The pine tree branches were still everywhere, almost like trees had grown inside the car. I pushed them out of the way so I could see…

There were Mom and Dad, exactly where we had left them. Their arms were in different positions. Their faces looked pale and their lips almost blue. Their eyes were closed. The blanket and some of the clothes we had piled on them were still covering them up.

"Mom! Dad!" I said. "I'm back. We got help for you!"

The van was silent. I could hear Butch coming down the hill, yelling at me: "Don't move them, Chapel! Don't move them!"

I wasn't going to move them, of course. I just wanted to know… well, you know.

Then Mom stirred. Just a little. I thought I saw a finger move under the blanket we had covered them with. And then her eyes flickered open.

"Chapel?" she said weakly. "Is everyone OK?"

"Everyone is fine," I said. "The fire department is here. An ambulance is coming."

"Oh, thank God," she said, and then she started to cry.

I saw Dad move his head a little. "Is Dad OK?" I said.

"He will be," Mom said. "He woke up once."

Butch was there by then. He leaned into the van, brushing aside a snow-covered clump of pine needles.

"Ma'am?" he said. "Can you hear me?"

Mom nodded, blinking back tears.

"You've got some very brave children," Butch said. "You're not going to believe what they went through. Now the cavalry is coming, OK? It's not just me. You understand? We're about to get a whole lot of help. We'll get you out of there. Everything is going to get better real soon. Now tell me first: Where are you hurt?"

But Mom didn't answer for a minute. She reached out for me, and I came closer, ducking my head further into the car so she could grab onto me. For once, I didn't mind being hugged. I felt one of her tears fall on the back of my neck.

"I was afraid we were never going to see you again," she said. "But you did it."

"It's OK, Mom," I said, burying my head into her and hugging her hard. "We're all going to be all right."

EPILOGUE

They called it "The Christmas Miracle" on TV and in the newspapers. We were big news for awhile – the four kids who had hiked 12 miles, scared off a bear and driven a truck to rescue their parents.

The ambulance arrived soon after Butch radioed exactly where we were. He asked Mom a lot of questions before they moved her – things I knew, like "Who's the president" and "What day is today?" – and then I saw them use something called "The Jaws of Life" to cut Mom and Dad out of the car. The Jaws of Life looked sort of like a huge pair of pliers, and at first I didn't think they could cut through a car.

"Can those really cut through metal?" I asked one of the rescue squad guys from the ambulance while he was deciding exactly where to slice into the van.

"Like a hot knife through butter," the guy said. "Don't worry – we practice with these on old cars all the time." And then they worked exactly like he said they would.

I rode back in the ambulance with Mom and Dad. Butch loaned us all of his firefighting gear in the truck to pile on top of them for extra warmth – they both felt ice cold, but the rescue workers said they would be OK. Butch went to go get the rest of the family, as well as Miss Swann, and then took them to the hospital waiting room. He even brought some of his own family out there for a while – he had two teenaged girls who spent most of their time looking down at their cell phones – as well as some of their Christmas dinner. We were glad for the company but gladder about the food.

By Christmas night, when my grandparents had gotten there, both Butch and Miss Swann felt like family.

Mom and Dad both stayed at the hospital for more than a week, but all the doctors said it could have been a lot worse. Mom had a broken leg and a few scrapes.

Dad had a broken leg too, along with a concussion, a separated shoulder and three broken ribs. They both had mild cases of frostbite. They were in wheelchairs together for several weeks. Then they hobbled around on crutches and then finally they mended well enough that, eventually, I could almost forget they had been hurt at all.

Our story happened on a slow news day, as Dad said. Christmas is one of those days where not much happens, he said, and every TV station and newspaper is looking for a nice story. At least that's what he told us, and I guess he knows, since that's his business. So we didn't just get in the newspapers. We got on TV, too — several camera crews came out and interviewed all of us, as well as Butch. By then, Georgia had learned how to say "May Rees-ras," which is all she said in her interview. She meant "Merry Christmas."

The TV story went national on CNN and a few other places. We got some nice letters from people who said we were an inspiration to kids. What we liked best, though, was an invitation from a place in California we had once heard of but never thought we'd be able to visit — an amusement park called "LegoLand." They wanted us to all come out there as their guests for a whole week — for free. And, they said we could also pick out anything we wanted from the Lego catalog. Somehow, they had heard in one of our interviews how much we liked Legos – especially me.

So we took them up on that.

We ended up becoming good friends with Miss Swann, too. We go to see her almost every time we go to see my grandparents now – although we don't ever take the blocked-off shortcut anymore. We go through Clarksville instead, and then double back. The reason she said she had been "waiting for Georgia" when we first met her, she has told us, is because she had seen a little girl that looked just like Georgia in her dreams. She said she had kept having the same dream once every week or so for three months before we came. In that dream, there was a small girl who suddenly appeared in her house and that Miss Swann knew she was supposed to help.

"Were we in the dream, too?" London asked the first time she told us this.

"You weren't there, child," Miss Swann said. "But Georgia was, and she looked exactly like she did the first day I saw her. In the dream, she toddled right into my sitting room one day after Arthur left, and she crawled right up on my lap. I said "What do you need, child?' And she said just one word. 'Help.'"

I wouldn't have believed that a year ago. But I do now. After all, I still believe the same fawn guided me to the wreck that had accidentally helped cause the wreck in the first place. My own personal shining star.

No one can be sure of that, but I know it's true. I was the first person to see the baby deer, and I was the last person to see the baby deer, and in between we Fowler Four had an adventure we would never forget.

THE END

Made in the USA
Coppell, TX
30 July 2020

31987942R00069